This Little Tiger book belongs to:

_____

_____

_____

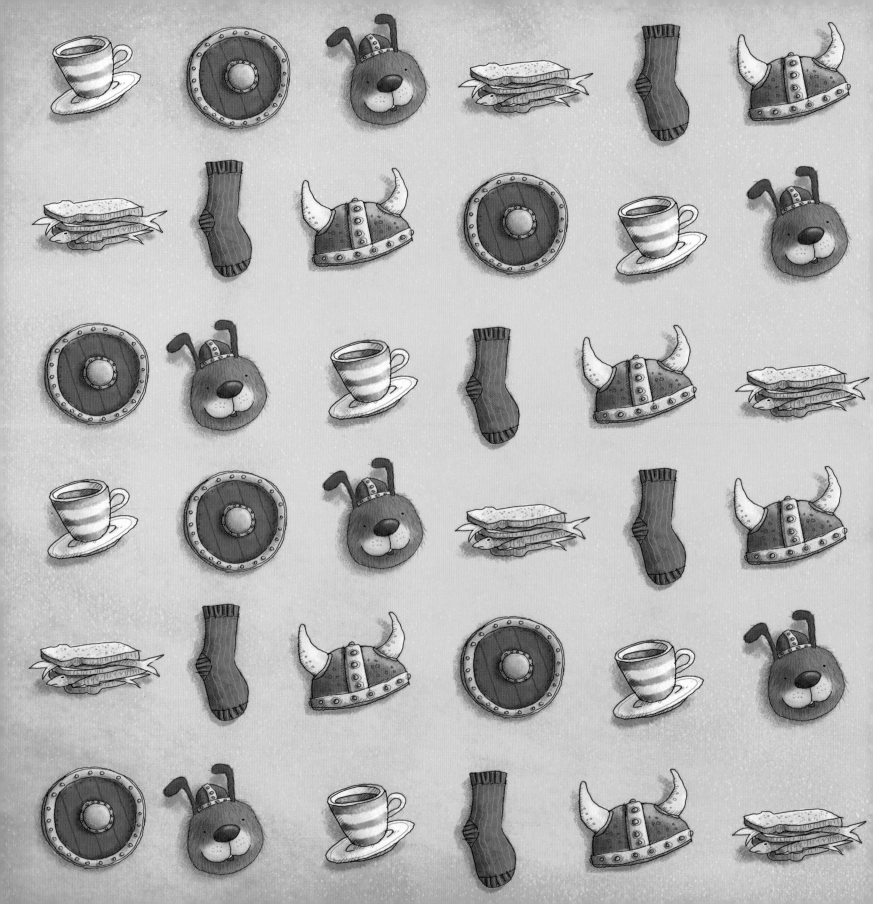

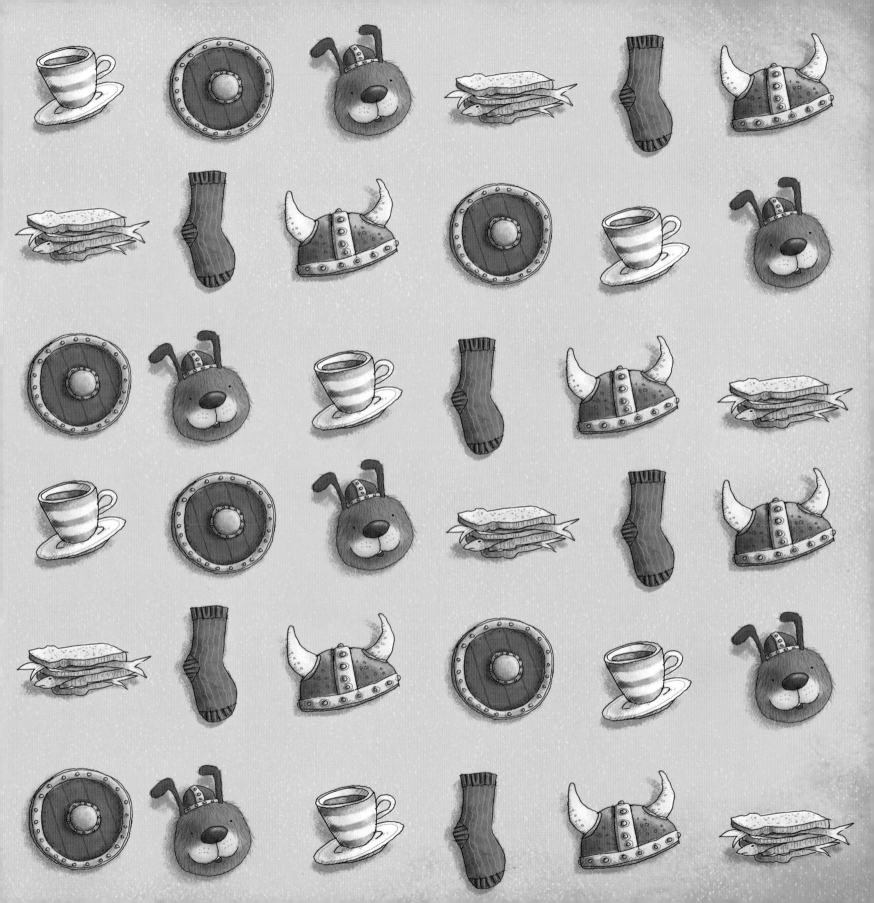

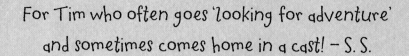

For Tim who often goes 'looking for adventure'
and sometimes comes home in a cast! – S. S.

To Laura, Grace and Oscar – L. W.

LITTLE TIGER PRESS LTD.
an imprint of the Little Tiger Group
1 The Coda Centre, 189 Munster Road, London SW6 6AW
www.littletiger.co.uk
First published in Great Britain 2010
This edition published 2017

by Steve Smallman   Illustrated by Lee Wildish

Dragon Stew

LITTLE TIGER
LONDON

Five bored Vikings went out hiking,
looking for adventure, but what could they do?
"Let's have a battle," said Grim, "or steal some cattle!"

"Let's go fishing in the dark for a massive, monster shark!"
suggested Bushi Bigbeard, but Harald hollered, "Poo!"

"Let's wrestle with a bear in just our underwear!"

But the other Vikings said,

"Well, THAT'S nothing new!"

"I'm really bored with hiking!" moaned Yop,
the grumpy Viking.
Then little Loggi Longsocks said,
"I know what we'll do.
We'll go and catch a dragon,
then tie it to a wagon,
then take it home and chop it
up and make a dragon stew!"

So they picked up the wagon that they needed for the dragon,
a stack of sardine sandwiches in case they missed their tea,
a fishing net, a ball of string, a pointy dragon-poking thing—
and stuffed them in a longboat and rowed it out to sea.

They sailed away together
through stormy winds and weather,
till a squelchy squeezy squid came
looking for a fight.

But one whiff of Harald's sock and the squid collapsed in shock.

And in no time all its tentacles were tied up good and tight.

Then Bushi grabbed the tail of a passing killer whale and said, "Take us to the dragon or we'll make a stew of YOU!"

ive happy Vikings went out hiking
on a fearless quest to catch
a dragon for their stew.

They tiptoed over logs
and they splashed
through squelchy bogs,

till they came across a gleaming,

steaming pile of . . .

DRAGON POO!

They hurried on until
they saw a knobbly, bobbly hill.
"Let's climb it!" Loggi Longsocks said.
"We'll get a better view!"
"Are we there yet?" grumbled Yop
as they struggled to the top.

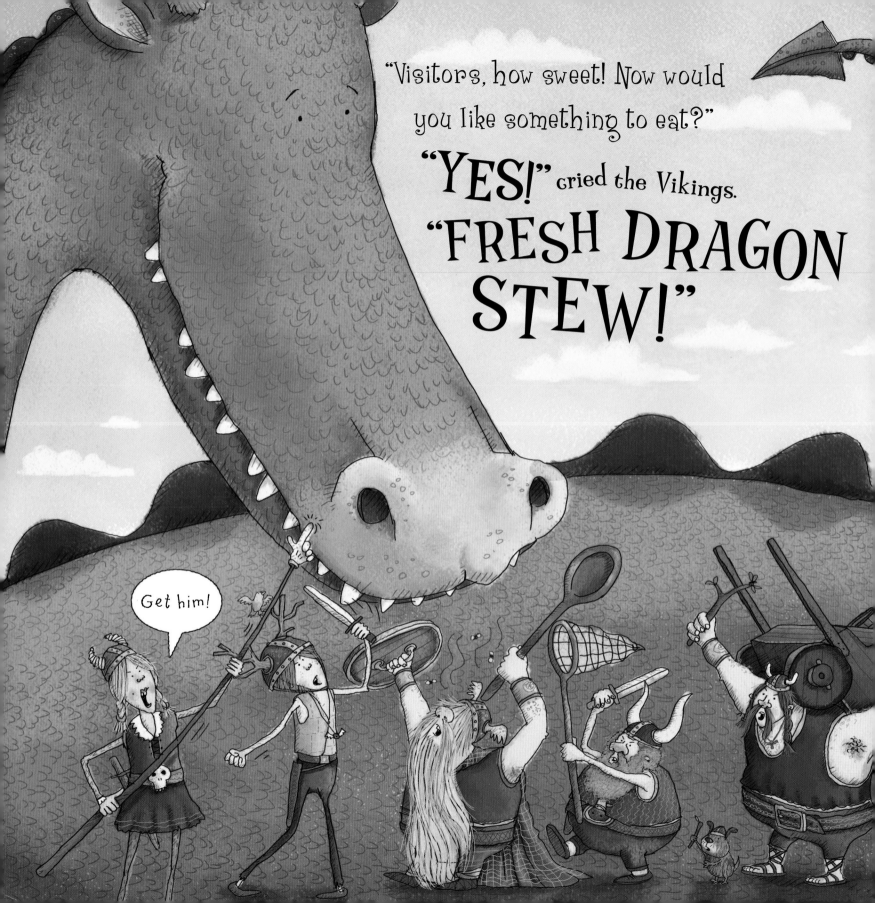

Then they started to attack him
and to poke him and to whack him.
And the dragon said,
"Oh, really, what a NASTY
thing to do!"

The dragon twitched his snout
and a jet of flame shot out.
It burst behind the Vikings
and set their pants alight!

Harald hollered, "HIDE!"
and Grim said, "MY BACKSIDE!"
And they legged it to their longboat
with their bottoms burning bright.

ive sore Vikings all quite liking
cooling off their bottoms in the sea so blue.
Harald said, "We're lucky—dragon probably tastes yucky!"

Phew!

Then Bushi roared, "I'm really bored!

SO, NOW WHAT CAN WE DO?"